The
STORY
of a
MOUSE

Published in 2008 by **JERBOA BOOKS**
PO BOX 333838 Dubai UAE
www.jerboabooks.com
ISBN 978-9948-431-65-7

Approved by the National Information Council UAE:
No 1540 27 December 2006

Text: © Denys Johnson-Davies
Illustrations: © Daniela Pellegrini

The
STORY
of a
MOUSE

by

DENYS JOHNSON DAVIES

Illustrations

DANIELA PELLEGRINI

This book would not have been possible
without the generous support of
Dubai Duty Free

ONCE UPON A time there was a holy man who lived with his wife in a small hut by the sea. One day as he was sitting in prayer by the shore a kite passed above him, carrying in its claws a small mouse. At that moment the bird let go of the mouse and it fell down and landed at the holy man's feet.

The holy man felt pity for this tiny creature, so he wrapped it up in a leaf and cared for it. When it was time for him to go home, he felt that his wife would find it difficult to look after such a small and weak creature, so he prayed to his Lord that it might be changed into a young girl.

In an instant the little mouse became a beautiful young girl. The holy man took the girl to his wife and said to her: 'This girl has been given to us to look after. Let us treat her as though she were our daughter.'

So the holy man and his wife took the young girl into their home.

Then the day came when the girl grew up. The holy man said to her, 'My child, the time has come for me to marry you to someone of your choosing, someone whom you love and can live with happily.'

The girl replied, 'If you allow me to choose my husband, then I would like him to be the strongest of all things in the universe.'

'Perhaps, then, you would like to have the sun as your husband?' the holy man suggested to her.

The holy man went to the sun and said to it, 'O mighty sun, I have a beautiful young daughter and she has asked to be married to the strongest of all things. You the sun are without doubt the strongest, so would you agree to marry her?'

But the sun answered, 'I am not the strongest of all things. I can show you something that is stronger than I. There is, for instance, the cloud that sometimes covers me and prevents my rays and their warmth from reaching the earth.'

The holy man then went to the cloud and told it what the sun had said about it being stronger. 'Would you, therefore, agree to marry my daughter?'

But the cloud answered, 'I am not the strongest of all things. I can show you something that is stronger than I. Go to the wind that has control of me and which can drive me here and there, to the west and to the east, just as it wishes.'

The holy man then went to the wind and told it what the cloud had said.

But the wind answered, 'I am not the strongest of things. I can show you something that is stronger than I. Go to the mountain which is so strong that I, the powerful wind, am unable to move it from its place.'

The holy man then went to the mountain and told it what had been said about it by the wind and asked it whether it would agree to marry his daughter.

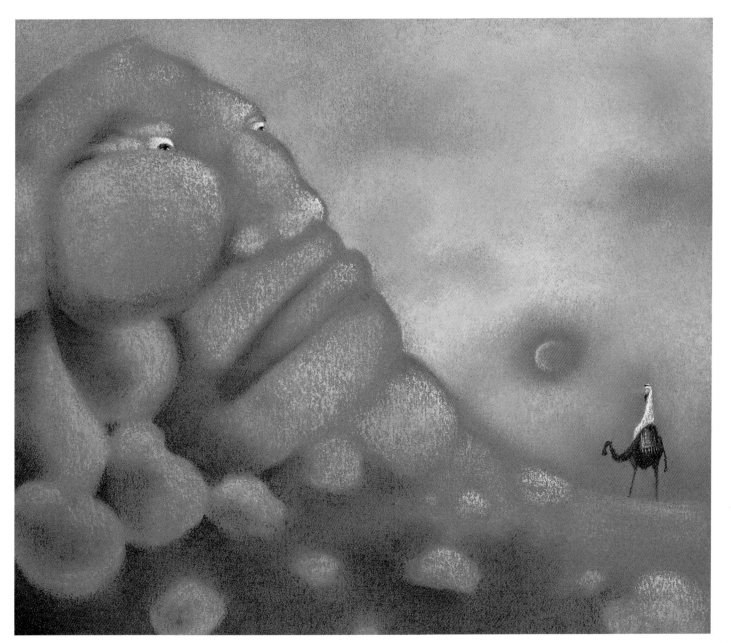

But the mountain answered him, 'I am not the strongest of all things. I can show you something that is stronger than I. Go to the mouse which makes a hole in my side as a home for itself. With all the strength that I have I cannot stop it from doing this to me.'

The holy man then went to the mouse and asked it, 'Will you marry this beautiful young daughter of mine?'

The mouse looked up at
the girl and answered, 'How
can I do that when the house I live in
is so small that this girl would not be able
to enter it. If I am to have a wife, then it is to a
female mouse that I must be married.'

So the holy man went to his daughter and told her
what had happened with the sun, the cloud, the wind
and the mountain.

'Daughter of mine, you wanted to be married to the strongest of things, but each one claimed that it was not the strongest. Now the mountain tells me that the mouse is stronger that it. What do you wish me to do about this?'

'If the mouse wishes to have me as his wife,' answered the girl, 'then please ask God to change me back into a mouse.'

So the holy man did as his daughter wanted and immediately the girl became once again a small mouse. After this she and the other mouse said goodbye to the holy man and his wife and went away to make a life together.

DENYS JOHNSON-DAVIES has been called 'The pioneer translator of modern Arabic literature.' Recently he published an anthology of Modern Arabic Literature. He is also the author of some fifty children's books.

The book 'Memories in Translation' tells the story of how he became interested in Arabic and provides amusing anecdotes about the many Arab writers he has known; the book is available in both English and Arabic. Denys received the Sheikh Zayed Award for 2007 as the Personality of the Year in recognition of his contribution to making Arabic literature known outside the Arab world. Jerboa Books has published a volume of his short stories under the title 'Open Season in Beirut.'

DANIELA PELLEGRINI is an Italian illustrator, born in Pesaro where she is also a social worker doing art workshops with people who have special needs. An award winning artist, this is Daniela's first commission for Jerboa Books.

Other children's books by Denys Johnson-Davies published by Jerboa Books

Tales of Arabia
    Deenoh and Arbab - A Story from the Emirates
    The King and his Three Daughters - A Story from Kuwait
    The Woodcutter - A Story from Qatar
    The Great Warrior Ali - A Story from Oman

The Tale of Two Donkeys
A Pair of Hoopoes
The Traveller
Foxy Tales Vol. 1